Something Said

Fiction & Verse

Mark Anthony Smith

For all the smiles on Twitter. You each make my day.

About the Author

MARK ANTHONY SMITH is the author of *Hearts of the Matter*, *Keep It Inside,* and *Brood.* He has since had poems and stories published in a range of small press magazines. Born in Hull, he continues to write horror for Red Cape Publishing and Demain.

Twitter: @MarkAnthonySm16

Website: www.markanthonysmith.com

Also available:

Hearts of the matter (CreateSpace)

Keep It Inside and Other Weird Tales (Red Cape Publishing)

Brood (Demain Publishing)

Acknowledgements

A big thank you to Cal Marcius at Spelk, Jaymes et. al. at Truly U, Julia Kosovo at Nymphs, David L O'Nan at Fevers..., J L Corbett at Idle Ink, everyone at Blue Animal, Mr. Simon Webster, Shane O'Halloran in Berlin, Thomas at Detritus, Chris at Alternative Stories and Fake Realities, Patricia M. Osborne, Nancy in Canada, Julia in London, Deborah Edgeley, Morgana at Fat Cat, David P Green, Ian Hairsine, Sean Haughton, Terry and Sue, Peter and Leanne at Red Cape, Dean and Adrian Baldwin at Demain, Squirrel E., anyone I haven't mentioned...and you.

Chitter Chatter was originally published in *Spelk* on 25th October 2019 - @SpelkFiction

The Scrimshaw Pipe was originally published in *Truly U* on 31st October 2019 - @Truly_U_

She Opens Doors was originally published in *Nymphs* on 28th November 2019 - @nymphswriting

A Sidewalk Romance was originally published in *Fevers of the Mind* on 14th January *La Petite Mort* 2020 - @FeversOf

was originally published in *Pink Plastic House* on 15th April 2020 - @pphatinyjournal

Tower of Strength was originally published in *Idle Ink* on 4th April 2020 - @_IdleInk_

The Hermit won first place and was originally published in *Blue Animal Literature* on November 4th 2019 - @BlueLiterature

Face Values was originally published in *The Cabinet of Heed* #29 on 22nd February 2020 - @CabinetOfHeed

Roundabouts was originally published in *Fiction Kitchen Berlin* on 25th January 2020 - @FictionBerlin

Deciduous, *Mollusc* and *Lasting Effects* were originally published in *Detritus* #3 on 31st December 2019 - @DetritusOnline

Another Meursault Death is unique to this collection.

The Velvet Ghost was originally published in *Ad Hoc Fiction* #188 on 4th December 2019 - @AdhocFiction

Cloud Animals and *At One* were originally published in *Be their voice: An Anthology for Rescue Volume 2* (CreateSpace) on 22nd December 2016.

Stick was originally published in *Patricia's Pen* on 24th November 2019 – www.patriciamosbornewriter.com

Make Up was originally published in *CommuterLit.com* on 4th March 2020 - @commuterlit

The 'Said Something' Monologue was originally published by *Musicians for Homeless* on the *Safe and Warm* CD on 9th January 2018.

Flowers for Whoever was originally published on *Paragraph Planet* on 21st October 2019 - @paragraphplanet

The Bear was originally published in *Nymphs* on 22nd January 2020 - @nymphswriting

The House They Talked About was originally published in *Fat Cat Magazine #2* on 15th February 2020 - @fatcatmagazine

The Man Who Stood There was originally published in Nymphs on 13th April 2020 @nymphswriting.

Present Presence was originally published in *Xmas Stories* on 13th February 2020 - @XmasIR

Christmas Eve and Hereafter was originally published in *Dodging The Rain* on 24th December 2019 - @dodgingtherain . It was reprinted in @XmasIR

An Early Resolution was originally published in *Xmas Stories* on 13th February 2020 - @XmasIR

We Can Order the Same or Taste Each Other's was originally published by *InkPantry* on 1st – 3rd April 2020 - @InkPantry.

Co

Chitter Chatter

Linda peels back the curtain. I can see the tiredness in her eyes now. She gazes out the window. 'I wish she wouldn't feed the birds,' she says. I watch her twist the Solitaire ring between thumb and forefinger. My wife is terminally ill with Cancer. She says, 'The birds make a mess everywhere.'

I often wonder about our elderly neighbour. She is rarely seen out and about. We can suppose that she is lonely. Feeding the pigeons and the sea gulls probably gives her some purpose in life. Someone once said, 'You'll never know until you ask her.'

Roy lives four houses away. He said he'd seen a rat stealing the bread that was scattered on the grass. 'The gulls gather on my roof and wake me up,' he shrugs. 'I've never really talked with her.' He remembers the street parties during the 80s. 'That was Community Spirit, was that.'

I wonder if the birds tell our neighbour all our secrets. Maybe the sparrows and blackbirds catch all the souls of people who've departed. Maybe she knows more than we think she does. 'You'll never know until you ask her.'

It seems a lot of people feel lonely now. Communities have changed and people move about more. Then there's shift work. We live in a 24 hour society. Sometimes, I'm on my phone as I pass those that live next door. I rarely recognise people now, I suppose.

On the morning that Linda died, there is the slightest knock on my door. I can barely move with shock and disbelief even though I thought I was prepared. There is that knock again. Then the letter box clatters: 'I'm Fiona from Number 84. I'm really sorry about Linda,' she calls. There is silence. Then, 'I used to be a Nurse.' It goes quiet. It is quiet as I think about the birds.

The Scrimshaw Pipe

I am not one to rock any boats but there's a dead pirate in my bed. His chest is certainly not falling or rising like Galleons did. The man also sleeps like a dead fish with blue tinged lips and awful hygiene. It's hard to keep yourself to yourself in these kind and few situations. My carpet is covered in dried bladderwrack and bits of bite-sized, deep sea corpses. The pincers of crabs, an odd urchin and something with tentacles like *Lovecraft's Cthulhu*.

I have visited Hull Maritime Museum a number of times and have never had the urge to leave with anything other than tourist leaflets and questions. The intricate whale bones were carved on long voyages to while away the hours. Some of them, furnished in soot to highlight the etchings, are art. And they speak to me. When I say, speak, I mean lull by song. They are like sirens luring sailors to a rocky death.

So, I didn't think a Scrimshaw pipe would be missed. How wrong was I to take it? How shocked am I to find something that wants them back? The faint figure awakes with a grimace. I doubt sleeping dogs will lie. The rotten figure rolls over and slumps to the floor. From sleep to an increased wakefulness, he gains strength and stature. I offer up the stolen artefact.

Yet, the pirate thing slaps them from my hand, and I feel sick. I am suddenly aware of my bowels. I offer entreaties as the bloated, toothless face opens its rotting maw to speak. I'm gasping for air at the stench of dead seafood. The eyes are without life as it struggles for words. Then, like a shipwreck, it rasps, "Give me your future!"

She Opens Doors

Even the downpour doesn't stop me from holding the door open. The kids file out of the burger joint with cardboard crowns and balloons into the vertical rain. I pull my sodden collar up. Their mother is shouting, 'Watch the cars!' Yet again, I'm not acknowledged. It really grinds me. Maybe, I'll just push past next time to dampen this rising anger in my chest. I was always told, 'Manners cost nothing, Nathan.'

I had a conversation twice. A lady with cropped blonde hair and too much make-up on said, 'I don't need a gentleman.' Then someone else wanted to help herself after mentioning something about Hegemonic Masculinity. What is it with everything today? And what do you do when you can't mind read? I resorted back to my old habits and hoped that I'd be thanked. Is that too much to ask? To be thanked for an act of kindness? I don't know. I know that things have changed since my parents' still mattered. Sisters are doing it, apparently... But I still have faith. Even if chivalry is outdated.

I choose several books in the bookshop that I can barely walk round. There are promotional tables everywhere. No-one looks or makes eye contact. They have their minds on a list of books that may or might not be stocked.

A woman with a rain jacket catches my eye in the crime section. I don't read crime as I prefer internal battles rather than plot. I try to read widely so nothing is lost. But I won't finish a book if I don't like the prose. And I don't read crime fiction. There are too many other tones to read. I'm not looking for anything in particular. They don't have the new literary prize winner in and I'm just waiting for the rain to stop, really. The lady has disappeared.

I choose a novella whose blurb mentions a renewed love affair and a paperback of prize-winning stories. I pay for a bag so the new books aren't likely to get covered in the shower gel I bought earlier. I don't expect a leak. I'm just precious about books. I would never fold a page to mark where I'd left off or lend my favourites to a friend. I try to keep them in alphabetical order and find it difficult to donate old ones to charity. I don't think I'm too precious about other things.

The rain has stopped and I have some new books. It is bright outside as I'm leaving the shop. I don't know why I turn. I'm not a mind reader. But turn I do as she heads out. I instinctively hold the door. It's that woman again with the purple hiking jacket. She says, 'Thank you.' I ask her if she likes crime. She laughs. 'Do I look dodgy?' Then, 'No. I don't really. It's a birthday present.' Then she reads my mind. Some women can. And after a coffee, I think that someone's life might change.

A Sidewalk Romance

Solid grey slabs
are sheened by the shortish
downpour that shimmers -
these blocks awash with the neon
signs that dance 'open'
outpours in sudden puddles.

Here, there
are splashes of worn splaying,
chewing gum or chalked
marks scrawling underfoot -
are they drawn to draw those niggles
away from the cracks?

Perhaps, you are shivering
or shaking that umbrella
when a weathered man or two
still holds onto values and holds
each door open.

The rain
trickles down the nape -
roused by a nodding gratitude.
Shop the Spring
sale if you will for
that special occasion to

be snapped from a future lover.
Then, perhaps, later you'll blow
to cool a green or Chai tea
and remember that we, once
hand in hand, had shared
the same hard pavement.

La Petite Mort

I knew you,
until tightest-lipped
you impressed my shoulder
with a tight chested
little death and then
I was pained.

You knew me,
until (un)certain days
became a pill-timed haze.
The times spent –
dissolved. And then
there's just (un)just blame.

Tower of Strength

I look up to the 17th floor. She is small and so high up. It would be easier to see her as a dot or a full stop. But she is subjective and coughing from the smoke. She has no choice. I cannot imagine what she is feeling. Maybe she isn't thinking at all.

I am helpless as she dangles the child. It must be such a hard decision. It must be difficult to say 'Goodbye' in a language the child would understand. I can barely hear the sobbing. She lets go of her bundle.

As the child free-falls to the ground, I have to wonder which is worse. Burning to death or dying on impact. I lose sight of her mother. She is lost in the smoke. The girl tumbles and I manage to catch her. "Everything will be alright," I say. But the words sound like someone else's.

The Hermit

The waves crashed drowning out the crunch of pebbles beneath my feet. It was bitterly cold and I was alone. I hadn't slept and my beard was a tangle like the stuff washed ashore. There were bits of discarded fishing tackle, broken shells and dried out seaweed along the shore. I straightened my woollen hat as my eyes narrowed.

The sun glinted off the smallest shell. It was a cream and bluish helix that had been smoothed by the waves. The horizon was vast but far off. I felt small. I pulled my collar up and walked over to the shell. Picking it up, it felt smooth and fragile. Yet it was a solid structure. I listened to the sea.

'You are a broken man. A shell of a man. Your ancestors crawled from the sea. Yes! From the sea you came and to the sea you must return.' It rushed with an age old wisdom. The knowledge of the moon and the tides. I thought about never feeling rooted. I have always drifted.

I removed my hat and coat. I felt small and inconsequential in this big wide world. The shell beckoned me. I succumbed. I crawled inside and felt at home. I was at peace as I waited for the tide to turn.

Face Values

This protects
in games or scares others
in the clammer of
your carnival disguise.
On a given day, another
might be part of that
beauty therapy – the mask that
opens pores. Through dual slits,
pressed above a moulded
mouthpiece, sometimes
this persona
takes away peace.
Sometimes, it horrifies
and takes away your
humanity. You become
that cheap object
like everything now. At least
knitted balaclavas
have, at face value, some
personalities. At least
you value your warm face.
Wear each loud or hide
inside to disguise the quiet one.

Roundabouts

She doesn't know if she should leave him. He has become too distant. Martin never looks at her when she tries to talk with him. He always has somewhere else he'd rather be. And now she has lost him at The Fair. Anne edges through the crowd past the food stands. The smell of fried onions and candy floss make her stomach turn. She hates crowds. She can't stand still and think. Everything is too bright. The lights on the rides, the noises, the screams and the laughter. She has to find him. Anne pushes through near the waltzers as they speed round and round.

Where could he be? She feels nauseous as she searches near the rollercoaster. It rattles up the track as it nears the summit before the winding drop. He isn't near the Ghost Train either with the gaudy paintings of werewolves and serial killers and the animatronic skeleton climbing up a rope with its red flashing eyes. The tall rides that loop the loop or spin upside down are always too much. Anne finds a space and throws up.

Martin was the perfect lover. He used to give her compliments and flowers. He used to listen and give her his full attention. Even her Mother liked him. But work has taken over and he has become more distant and aloof. He isn't as funny as he used to be.

She rarely smiles now. He's changed. That much was true. And Anne feels quite alone, even now, through the crowds.

She looks again past the food stands. Anne's breathing is shallow. She is growing impatient. The candy floss and fried onions mingles like something sour and sweet. The lights affect her ability to see in the dark as she listens to the banter and notices a Fortune teller. The Romany lady in black beckons at the door of her caravan. Anne does not make eye contact. She doesn't want a contract or an obligation because she finds it hard to say no. The clacking of rides and screams and laughter feels like an onslaught on her senses. She wants to go home. She wants Martin to stand still and acknowledge her. She needs to find him. Would she leave him?

The rollercoaster is climbing again. It must have done a lap or two. It went on and rattled without her being there to observe it. All this would be gone soon. The rides would move on somewhere else and the rubbish would be swept away. It would be just a car park again at the end of the week. She acknowledges the feeling of loss. She needs to focus. He isn't near the Ghost Train with the serial killers in masks or the skeleton with red flashing eyes that flashed. It's the same as before. Her repeated search is becoming as fruitless as the first. But she can't stop. Not now. Even as she wants to stand still and think. Her mind is spinning.

Then, she jumps as someone tapped her shoulder. She spins off kilter. There is the familiar face who looks as perturbed as ever. He says, 'We really can't go on like this.'

And for a moment, Anne stands still.

Deciduous

These days
prolonged with clocks
going back. Each self
recedes as leaves.

That matured
canopies bear these
Wintered saps –
exposed, unhealed, relieved.

Mollusc

The snail retracts into its shell as I pluck it from the silvery line on the plant pot. Was this a conscious withdrawal from the world or a stimulus response to danger?

I find myself sucked in to a very different place as the mollusc accommodates me in its calcium-rich retreat. It isn't the slickest or most spacious of places but everything slows down in our new home.

Lasting Effects

Of course, the old house, that everyone crosses the road to pass by, isn't haunted. Me and Spud check the cobwebs and shadows ourselves. I just wish we had closed the front door on our way out.

My hand is fine, at first. There is nothing reptilious or peeling about it. Then Spud texts and texts me. 'My hand has a life of its own,' he said. Now the house calls him back and my own body is not my own.

Another Meursault Death

There was another 'Meursault death' yesterday. It's happening too often now. Dressed like Camus's Arab, the perpetrator strangled a passer-by simply because it was too hot. The sun is an oppressive orb in the sky and society is turning nocturnal. Most of The United Kingdom is barren. Its coast erodes quicker with rising sea-levels. Some of East Anglia is resigned to memories. Not that people remember much. They're living for the moment now.

"I can't see your face, son." Keith is sat by Rutland Water with his six-year-old grandson. Ethan's eyes are wide as he loosens his cowl. "You used to fish here?" They looked out onto the creeping desert. "We did," the old man replied. He fights back a tear. "I wanted you to catch a carp too." Ethan understands the tone. He tries to settle for a story but a Vitamin D deficiency makes him listless.

"People were more bothered about fighting with others. They wanted to ban the Burkha. We were more bothered about the outsiders than we were about holding the authorities to account." Keith licks his cracked lips. "We denied the climate change warnings until it was too late. Then it was too late."

"Oh! Me and the lads used to pack up and fish

here for hours. We caught some whoppers. On days we didn't land anything, it was okay. We had a laugh. Catching a fish was a bonus. I wish you could have been there." Ethan's dull eyes widened. "First, the hosepipe bans became more regular. Then they were the norm. Our gardens began to wither. Water became gold."

"The earth has always revolved through hot and cold spells if you look at geological time. But this was normalised in the face of growing evidence. We lived through disinformation and fake news. Everyone was right and everyone was wrong. Global commerce took its toll. It depleted the Earth's resources. What is funny is that as we set about those with different cultures, we became more homogenous. We became them. We even dress like them now, Ethan."

Ethan looked beyond the waste and smiled a child's smile. There was nothing on the horizon to describe or talk about. Yet here they were talking. "Is it all bad, Grandad?" Keith smiled. He patted Ethan's shoulder. "I'll have to think about that, Son. Come on, it's 62 degrees, your Mam will be getting up soon. The night is looming."

They passed the burnt-out cars whose hulks were like rusted dinosaurs. Many people cooked on the scrapped bonnets. There were a few trees which barely resembled what they were. It was always dangerous to be 'out and about.' People were

28

desperate. They were driven out of their minds with dehydration and the heat. Most of the societies – society had fragmented – lived at night. They had adapted to their surroundings that had changed through collective ignorance.

Keith chuckled. "It's not all bad," he says. "We have to cover up ourselves because of the cover ups. But people band together. They do. They find ways forward. Yes. People band together."

The Velvet Ghost

"Who's there?"

I have been six years without sight. Someone has let their self into my home. My nose and ears compensate my eyes. I hear the dog dish being stumbled over. No doubt there's biscuits all over the kitchen floor. I reach for my guide stick.

"Who's there?" My chest is tight and I feel my breath evading me as I try to swallow. Will I be beaten in my own home? Will they take what little is left? I am alone since Margaret passed on. The intruder is passing my sideboard. I can hear the dried petals crunch underfoot. The plants need a good watering. I start to ease myself from my chair to confront the unseen shade that challenges me.

A cold, velvet touch caresses my cheek. My brow furrows as I become weightless. I recognise her. It's a woman's touch. Her hand is cold but familiar.

Cloud Animals

Raking blades
apart, on knees, we
disagreed. To tame the tiger;
to frame the bees.

Under bonnets –
mostly. We felt the love.
Differences aired,
hands in glove.

But when love is
solid like ancient fates
weighted, it slides from
grips then dissipates.

Oh! Unclouded elephants
of the skies. Imagine
trunks; the feat! We sigh
as close allies.

At One

The awkward tot
whoops at something
kitten-like and quick.

Her beaming smile
belies time through
timelessness.

Only children and
animals playfully inhabit the
furry, blurred wordless world
where cats can be dogs
and dogs can be cats and
children can dream forever.

Stick

My stockier, older brother is stuck in the woods. He has twisted his ankle and is in pain.

I remember my pain as he twisted my arm behind my back. I remember crying out as he hit me and pinned me down for borrowing his bike without asking. For once, I am stronger than him.

I pick up a thick stick from the branches strewn about. I feel the weight as I tap it against my leg. Should I think about the consequences? The anger that I've hidden repeatedly rises in my chest.

I barely recognise those terrified eyes.

Make Up

She's too old for her Dad now. Both daughters are. They think I'm about 97. I'm much younger than that. I just don't keep up with today's music. Some people say I'm lost in the '90s. But I just worry about Cara. At 14, she shouldn't spend so much time in her room. She should be out with her friends. I worry about her getting depressed. She's always on that damned phone and she barely talks to me.

I always played with both my girls when they were at Primary school. They loved their woodland animal figures that drove an ambulance or a bus. Then they progressed onto adult games. I'd get into trouble for talking 'in class' whilst the white board was filled with spellings. Then we'd bake a cake with building bricks or play 'shops.' We sometimes fell out. We always did. "I'm not your friend. I'm your Dad." She'd pout and reply, "I don't like you." I'd return, "Good! I'm not paid to be liked." It was similar to now. She isn't talking to me now.

I wish she'd read or draw or create. But Cara just texts boys on her phone or scolds her school friends. I can't understand how she has so much to say when she's seen them at school all day. She's not interested in taking up a new hobby or reading a book.

Cara files out of her bedroom with her arms full. She gets a second lot of make up. "This palette is limited edition. You put it on with this brush. No! That brush is just for show. Smell this! It smells like cocoa." I smile and nod. I nod and smile. I know I'm not really following the application tutorial. I'm thinking about when Cara wanted her Dad as a child before she was 'growing up.' Now, I relish any time she finds for me. Even if it means falling behind with make-up.

"I just want you to be safe on-line," I say. "You never know who you're talking with. And if he asks you for any rude pictures..." Cara cuts in, "I know, Dad." I smile. My Baby is a young woman. "So, are you talking to your Dad now?" She laughs and shows me her dhobi brushes again.

The 'Said Something' Monologue

I need to feel warmth as the sun thaws your back to remind me of that shared humanity. But your fixed stare, seen before, fixes North or elsewhere. It glances 'just above minus.' You tense up, stride past, then unzip your jacket as the 'cold snap' melts away.

I might have nodded, said "Good morning" or proffered a smile. Someone could have moved it along with a few coppers before the coppers came. But you're too far away and my cheek feels like dank pavement. The climate wasn't open to small change or a bigger difference.

You recede. She approaches. She smiles and I'm sure something is going to change.

Flowers for whoever

'Oh, they're lovely,' beams Anna. 'You go to such lengths to make me feel special.' She looks at Tom with reddened eyes as she holds back tears and draws in the yellow, red and orange carnations through her nostrils.

Then, she goes to fetch her favourite vase from the kitchen. She starts trimming the stalks and arranges the rainbow array of scented happiness. It's a cheerful scene until she reads the card.

'Who's Laura?'

The Bear

The coffee at the Platform Buffet is far too expensive so we wait on the cold green, cast-iron bench without a drink. The train shouldn't be too long anyway. I look at my son with his ragged bear. He takes him everywhere but has yet to give the soft toy a name. Since he started Primary School, earlier this year, Phillip has become far more argumentative. He'll be five soon. We sit and wait on Platform 2. I ruffle the boy's hair as he talks to his bear.

There's a man on the opposite platform drinking from a disposable cup. The steam rises as he removes the lid to cool his drink. He looks at his watch and I'm sure I recognise him. I think about shouting over. The name 'Simon' is on my lips. Then he looks up. He isn't the man I know from working in the assorted sweets factory. I feel embarrassment. There's the memory of the taste of liquorice somewhere in my mouth. Then I look away.

I think about train journeys where I'd passed several stations without realising we'd passed them. The novel soon becomes habitual, I think. Phillip's Dad and I had bought our son the bear when he was born. He was so small then. Our son clung so tightly to the bear when his Dad finally left. Our love had grown cold as our baby needed attentions. Phillip's Dad was never one for kids. But he didn't really know that until it was too late. He didn't want to grow up.

I really want a cigarette. The wind blows through the exposed platform as it whips up leaves. I smile at the thought of excuses for train delays. Phillip is looking into the bear's eyes and telling him about Grandma. "If we're good there'll be sweets and cake. Yes! As much cake as you can eat! But you mustn't go through her cupboards." I smile. Phillip always drags my Mum's pots and pans out. He always makes a mess and she never has the patience for him.

I look at my watch whilst shuffling my feet to keep warm. "Mummy?" I look to the right.

"It's coming Phillip. Come on!" The train rolls in. I grab his shoulder as the doors open. A few people get off with suitcases and look relieved or confused. Then we step aboard the carriage and I steer Phillip to the left. We find our reserved seats on the quiet coach. Phillip sits by the window. I am just putting our small bag in the overhead compartment when he starts to cry. "What's the matter?" He sobs, "I haven't got Bear." I calm him then tell him to wait.

I hurry off to the bench on the platform. There are still passengers alighting with suitcases. The man with the cup is sat where we had sat. "Excuse me? That's our bear," I almost apologise. The man, quite alone, looks up. "Oh! You're quite mistaken," he frowns, "I bought this bear in Rhyll." I can feel my anger rising. "No! It really is our bear." I look at Phillip for some kind of reassurance. He bangs on the window with his small fist. His words are silent. Then the train pulls away and I really feel the cold.

The House They Talked About

I try to follow her lesson, story, conversation or occasional remonstration but it's easy to become distracted. My father left soon after he first clapped eyes on me. I rarely see anyone but my mother. Indeed, everything I know about the outside world comes from her teachings. She says, 'Henry. You're the apple of my eye.' I like to try to please her so she pulls me tight and I feel secure against her bosom. Other people, as I've listened from the top of the stairs, have called me a bad apple. But Mother tells me not to worry.

My mother says our neighbours spread rumours throughout our small village. We live near the forest and I love to hear the shaking of the trees against the fortified walls. The rhythms slow my heart and I feel good about that. The trees are as old as the moon and the stories my mother tells me.

The first settlers here, shaped our village from the natural habitat. The houses were built from local stone and wood from the pine forest. The place grew and grew with new folk. They brought new technologies such as the wheel and the crucifix. Soon, the folk started to change. Things were moving too fast. So, they built a wall and left the world outside. No-one was allowed through the closely guarded gates. When people became sick they would not call for outside help. All knowledge was contained within. My mother has described what a book is but I have never seen one because they're rare.

Mother came from the forest. She still talks about how they used to live. That was before the village. They hunted and lived off the land. She was still fearsome, to others, in her older age. The others respect her bulky pelt with her taut sinews. She is much respected for putting our village elder underground. He was the one that civilised my parents. But teaching them to use a knife and fork was too much. Since, she dispatched him, my mother is more melancholic. She decided eventually to embrace some new tools and worked the land.

I've often looked out onto our well-tended garden. There are flowers as far as the eye can see. I love the roses and the sunflowers and the weeping willow. I want to explore the shed that my Father built but I don't want to upset the apple cart.

They say that my mother cut my father's throat as he slept – right across the Adam's apple. I don't believe there's a grain of truth in that. Others say he left the village and returned with something that would contaminate us. They say he was imprisoned after the object he carried was removed. I have often thought about him.

There is nothing in our house that belonged to my father. Just the shed remains. But my mother says, 'Henry. You must never go outside.'

My nails are sharp as I scratch my head. I am sure that there's nothing to fear. My mother is in the front garden as I peek at the shed out back. I gulp the biggest gulp and decide to take a quick look in Father's shed. I feel clumsy as I descend our stairs as it's something I rarely do. My over-sized feet are unsteady on my pale legs. I need to cut my toenails.

The back door is too loud as I fumble with the lock. My heart is thumping my chest. I run past through the well-tended garden to the shed in all its decay. The door is unhinged and rotting and weathered. I push what remains to enter the gloom inside. I see a broken reflection and I scream such as no human throat can. There's something huddled in the corner. But Mother is here to take it all away.

The Man Who Stood There

She feels her chest tighten as the man looks on. He does nothing. Theresa approaches the elderly woman who is stuffing packets of rice and tinned fish down her blue coat. The woman is shaking. "I'm sorry," she shakes before making eye contact. Then her face relaxes. Her eyes well up with tears. Theresa leans in and whispers, "Put them back, eh?" The woman fumbles with the things she has taken and acts fast as she empties her pockets. "I'm not a bad person," the woman continues. Theresa agrees, refusing to call her for what she is – a shoplifter. She gives the lady a twenty-pound note. The woman can't thank her enough. She must be desperate.

The woman disappears. Theresa sees her again with a shopping basket. She is smiling as she puts a loaf of bread in. Then, Theresa sees the long queue and the lone shop assistant. She sees the second empty till. Elsewhere, a man is standing there. He is doing nothing. Theresa can see he spends time at the gym. But she tries not to be judgmental about his lack of empathy. She tries to normalise her angry thoughts but they cannot reconcile. Someone who waits in the line calls out angrily. He is mock looking at his watch for emphasis. Another man mumbles something about "patience." The shop assistant finally reaches under the counter. The bell rings and a colleague slopes out from out the back. The man is leafing through a life-style magazine.

Theresa stands in the diminishing queue. The shop assistants are talking to each other about a Christmas staff night out. The woman in the blue coat joins the queue behind Theresa. Her name is Susan. "Thank you," she says again. "I get paid tomorrow." Theresa talks. She recalls times with little money. Susan smiles. "I come in here a lot," she offers. Theresa nods and pays for her groceries and a lottery ticket.

She is leaving the shop. What sort of man does nothing? Does he even vote? Would he help a child who has fallen off her bike and has grazed her knee? Theresa sighs as she feels angry. Then she feels an urge. She nervously re-enters the convenience shop. The man is still at the magazine rack. Does he not know that his actions matter? Does he not know that he can make a difference to someone else's life? Theresa's bags are heavy. She approaches the man. Clearing her throat, she looks towards him but not at his face. He stands tall. This is not something Theresa does. The man looks angry. "Did you feel nothing?"

He looks at Theresa and drops his guard. He thinks. He pops the magazine back. Then he stands back. He takes in her whole stature instead of just her breasts. "It was really kind what you did," he says. Theresa feels her shopping lighten. The plastic handles aren't biting her palms as much. "Your actions have given me faith in humanity again." Theresa reddens. She wasn't expecting a compliment. "I'm Phil," he smiles. They talk and then later they might talk again.

Present Presence

'But it's not lying when you tell them that Santa exists,' said Mary. 'Would you like some more roast potatoes?' Ken looks at her husband who nods for him to help himself. Ken thanks Mary and has to restrain himself from scooping too many spuds onto his plate. He is famished and all too aware of the ingrained grime on his hands. 'I'll trim your beard later,' Peter pipes up. Mary nods at Ken who smiles. He feels better after the bath already. 'Tell us what happened!'

Ken looks at their teenage children. They are old enough to know that Santa didn't exist anymore. He finishes a potato roasted in goose fat and continues, 'I had it all,' he said. 'Then I lost it last Christmas.' The family leans closer. Ken continues, 'I worked at the department store for eighteen years. Last year, they asked me to cover the Santa's Grotto. I thought it'd spread some cheer. But one of the children pulled my beard away. She cried that Father Christmas was fake and didn't exist. Her parents got really angry and I lost my temper.'

'So you became homeless?' Ken nods. He smiles at how the smallest action can have the biggest consequences. 'Yes. Within three months of losing my job, I was evicted and 1 had nowhere to go.' There was a long silence. Ken looks at the brightly decorated tree and all the presents underneath it. He listens to the scraping of cutlery as turkey and beef is cut. Mary clears her throat.

Father Christmas does exist,' she smiles. 'He lives in the spirit of giving. It's not a lie. Not at all!'

Ken shudders as his eyes widen. He is thankful that this family has offered him some Christmas dinner. It was cold in the shop doorway where he'd huddled. He smiles and thanks her. He thanks them all for their kindness. Then Peter pipes up, 'You needn't go back out there. Not tonight. And I'll speak with the manager at the hostel tomorrow. We'll get you sorted!' Ken wipes the tears from his eyes.

'Now. Who's got room for pudding?'

Christmas Eve and Hereafter

He is excited, bathed
and tucked up in warm sheets
of lavender whilst
the candled scent of
mulled wine burns
downstairs
in front of the telly.

The boy cannot settle
as the snow outside is
heavy like the expectations
in his chest. He is
thinking about unwrapping
new gifts, in the morning,
to fill his toy box.

He finally drifts
before reindeer bells
settle on the roof. Someone
in happy dreams takes
the cookies and milk
then leaves
memories wrapped
under the tree.

An Early Resolution

Huw took a long drag and inhaled the smoke. He really could not give this up. It was one of his guilty pleasures. "I'll give up meat," he called from the back door. "That's my New Year's Resolution." Trisha whooped. "I'll hold you to that." He took another lungful, shuddered, dotted his cigarette out and closed the door. It was cold.

Huw could smell the joint wafting from the oven. He closed his eyes as his stomach rumbled. Potatoes roasted in goose fat, Yorkshire puddings, beef and loads of gravy. Trisha had even bought some Horseradish sauce. Huw gulped. Then the phone rang. Trisha was having a lay down after her Night shift at the hospital.

Huw picked up the receiver to his mother. Her central heating was down and Bubbles needed to go to the vets. Dad was at the pub again. There was nothing on telly. Huw told her that he was supporting Trisha and becoming a vegetarian in The New Year. His mam was supportive for once. She extolled the virtues of a healthy diet in helping her diabetes. Then she mentioned Huw's sister's kids. His nephew had been banned from school dinners at nursery and had to take sandwiches instead.

Trisha stomped down the stairs. "What's that burning?" Huw jumped up. The kitchen was full of smoke. "I'll have to go," he barked down the receiver. The beef was beyond saving. A blackened crust outweighed the tender meat. He couldn't eat that. The girls came back for their dinners. "Shut the door. It's freezing!" Trisha giggled. "Well, you can't eat that," she said, "but there's plenty of vegetables."

We Can Order the Same or Taste Each Other's

A novella about food and love

For Squirrel – with lots of love and sunshine

Menu
Sausage rolls
Scrambled Eggs and Mushrooms
Veggie Supreme Pizza
Enchilada
Smashed Avocado
Pre-packed Salmon Sandwiches
Shepherd's Pie
Carrot Cake
Beef Stew
The Full English
Spinach
Haddock and Chips
Macaroons
Cheese and Ham Baguette
Spiced Lentil Soup
Coleslaw Wrap
Vegetable Samosas
A Chocolate Rabbit
Baklava
Nil by Mouth
Angel Delight

Sausage Rolls

As a girl, I can't see her now. Sometimes, I think I can see her back then. But memories are fuzzy things. They are elusive or become mixed up with something else. Some of my reminisces are concrete. They are set in a strong emotion like the first time I was mesmerized by a Spaceship on the big screen. Others are composites like a cut-and-paste photo-shop. Try as I might, I cannot take myself back to my school days. I can't see Marie in the school dinner queue as she ritually pays for her daily sausage roll and beans. That is the only constant from all those years ago. That we both ordered the same for our dinner each day. I didn't know this, then. It's only since talking with her that we realised we ordered the same school dinners. I look back.

Marie says she was quiet at school. It's hard to imagine her like that. She did well and she didn't like boys. They were too angry all the time. She is a lot more confident now in her mid-40's. I still see her vulnerabilities, at times, but mostly, she finds an answer to most problems. I look at our recent photos. We are always happy together. And I tell Marie that she could pass for three or four different women depending on how she wears her hair or the angle from which the snap was taken.

She's changed a lot since how I vaguely

remember her outside the classroom in her school uniform. Her hair is longer and she's a lot chattier. Marie is a manager at a fashion company. I think that has brought her out of her shell a bit. That, and the passing of time. She's had children too. So have I. Two girls who are now at secondary school. They're at the ages when I first knew Marie. I can't really picture her.

We eventually left school and went our separate ways. I joined The Army and Marie went to college. I never thought I'd ever meet her again. Nor did that question even enter my mind. I didn't think about her. Then, she came back into my life thirty years later as I try to recall how she was at school. But I can't really. I must have bumped into the teenage Marie. I'm sure I did. I just can't think of a concrete situation where that happened. I just vaguely recall seeing her sometime, from recognising her back then, from an old school photograph. I want to think that I've always been there for her. But I'm sure she existed for thirty years without me. She probably didn't even give me a second thought as I went through Army Basic Training.

Now she has come back into my life, I don't want us to go our separate ways again. I want to think that she is my one constant in this ever-changing world. All those years ago, we ordered the same school dinners.

Scrambled Eggs and Mushrooms

I remember Marie seeing my newspaper article on social media. That's when she contacted me and offered her help. She lives down South. But she could organise a supermarket delivery if I was short of food. I felt really blown away by her generosity. She always helps other people and she tries not to judge.

I remember us, much later, walking past a homeless guy. I was in pain and wanted to go home. I felt angry with myself because I had little patience. Sometimes, I give someone in need some change. But I was skint. He was the public face of The Government's Social Policies. I wanted to feel angry at the politicians yet they are faceless. So, the vulnerable people, on the streets, take the wrath instead. It's not usually their faults. The notion of a Meritocracy is a myth. I had to be reminded of this as Marie found time for him.

The homeless guy was called David. He had been a successful musician until he went bankrupt because of a few accidents at a gig. He hadn't seen his children for six years. He said it was tough. Marie made him smile. She gave him some change too and never questioned whether he'd spend it on drugs or alcohol. "Live and let live," she said. I agreed.

That's the trouble with people nowadays. They don't realise that a smile can make a difference. I try to smile and say, "Hello," even when I'm in pains. It might be the only warmth someone has received that day. I try to make a small difference to others. Marie agrees. It's the small gestures that make a big difference. I just get really annoyed that people see my pains but don't make allowances for my unseen disability. They carry on talking even as I've lost the thread. I can't keep up.

Marie saw past the difficulties reported in the newspaper article. She said I wasn't weak at all. I was strong because I was standing up for others as I added my 'case study' to the mounting evidence. Those with disabilities are struggling like the increased homeless folk. Marie said, "don't look at what you can't do. Look at what you can." Her understanding was like a ladder that lifted me out of a pit of unending days. I could look forward to her video calls. She made me feel sexy again. She genuinely listened and I was her sounding board. She never judged me. Her scrambled eggs tasted good. I wasn't in the dark like a mushroom. Marie gave me my appetite back. I learned to love my world again as I adjusted. And Marie expanded the premature end to my travels by taking me with her when she video phoned.

It feels like fate. She is exactly the right woman to come into my life at exactly the right time. I began asking questions. I am still in pains but the world is new as I have lost my preconceptions about other's appearances. Marie has awoken me. Her interest makes me question and listen again. It feels like a good thing.

Veggie Supreme Pizza

She doesn't like the ways animals are treated. I went without meat for two days but wanted to gnaw someone's leg off. I said I'd never eat meat if we ever lived together. I felt trepidation after saying this. I'm not sure I could stick to Marie's principles. I like pork too much. We share a Veggie Supreme Pizza for tea.

Marie tells me about cows that are constantly impregnated to produce milk. I find that horrifying too. And she is nervous about confined spaces. We didn't dwell on battery hen conditions. That can't be a good life. Being cooped up in a small cage. I'm not sure chickens know any different though. We should be more ethical towards life.

I agree that all life is equal. But I believe in God. Man was made flesh to rule over the earth. So, I think all lives are equal. But only mankind was made in God's image. That makes us his highest creation. But with knowledge comes responsibilities. So, just because we can cage a bird, it doesn't mean we should. There is plenty of space to let farmed animals roam. It's about maximum profit, I tell Marie.

"You believe in God?" I tell her I do. Nothing is an accident. There's too much order about for our Universe to just be the effect of a random explosion.

You only have to look at the beauty of a rose to see that there's a creator behind it. And I don't think that when our physical body dies that that is the end. We live on, I'm sure. We have the capacity to love and think up poetry. I'm sure those attributes don't die when our proteins wither. Einstein said that energy can not be created or destroyed. I think we just take on another form.

I said to Marie that if I go first, I'll look out for her. In death, I will order her toiletries and find her car keys. I'll fold her clothes and stop her if she doesn't see the car as she's crossing the road. I will always watch over her. She thinks that's sweet. "But don't you think it's a bit creepy?" I think.

It's true that I'm quite a private chap. I struggle to use public loos if there's other people about. And I'm quite tactile in a relationship. But I don't need to see my girlfriend's ablutions or watch her shave her legs. I think about this. Or rather, I try not to. "OK," I say, "Then I'll always be within ear shot." We both laugh.

Marie thinks there's something more but she hasn't made her mind up as much as I have. She asks me to explain God and I struggle. Not everything can be explained. If I knew all the answers then I'd be God-like. But I'm only made in his image. I'm not totally sure what that means. God is male. And yet women are made in the image of our Heavenly Father too. I think it's more to do with the Trinity. So, it's less about appearance because our eyes can deceive us. We rely too much on our eyes at the expense of our other senses. I think 'in his image' means we have a spirit and a soul as well as a consciousness. But I'm not all knowing. I don't need to know everything. Love doesn't need to be quantified to be looked on with awe.

Enchilada

Marie looks beautiful as we go on our first date. She calls it dinner even though she's a Northerner. It sounds more formal than tea. She knows I have my dinner at mid-day. This is an on-going joke as I begin to sound 'di...' before I mock correct myself with tea. We go out to eat anyway. She chooses a Mexican restaurant.

She is wearing a short-sleeved dress that I say looks oriental. The eatery is busy. We find a table for two near the window that looks out onto the street. I already know I'll order a latte. Marie looks at the vegetarian options. I watch her as she traces the menu with her index finger and looks flummoxed. "I'll order the same as you," I say. She smiles. "You don't have to order the vegetarian option. You like your meat." She decides on a green mojito and a vegetarian Enchilada made with mushrooms.

"But I want the same experience," I remark. I talk about travelling alone, which is fine, although there is no-one to share the experiences with. Photos only go so far in painting a conversational picture. She listens. "Well, we can order the same or taste each other's," she suggests.

I order a latte and a burrito filled with ground beef. Marie won't try mine. The portions are large and we end up taking half of it with us when we leave. It is really busy and I'm in pains. She helps me through the weave of tables. I think about the connotations and we laugh at something private.

Smashed Avocado

Marie orders smashed avocado on toast for breakfast. I quite like them. I'm not sure if avocadoes are an aphrodisiac but I really don't need a chemical high to feel aroused when she's about.

There's a mother berating her kids. She seems unaware of other customers as she swears and tugs at the boy's hood. I tut. Marie says that she'd never talk to her girls like that. "Some people lack empathy and awareness for those around them." I say it's because everyone wants to be a celebrity. But, in truth, it's probably more to do with socialization and parents. Either way, social media pulls people away from parenting and promotes people who are famous just for being famous. I drift.

"Have you ever had a car accident?" I mention the time a woman pulls out in front of me from a junction. She said she didn't see me because the sun was in her eyes. Luckily, I was only doing thirty miles per hour. But she wrote my car off. I was alright. But the lady had popped home twice whilst I was waiting for the recovery vehicle and she didn't even offer me a drink. "Again. That's a lack of empathy," I say. I ask if Marie has ever had a car accident.

Marie tells me about the time, in her twenties,

before having children, that she skidded and her car left the ground. Her scarf had been cut in two by the shattered windscreen. She was lucky not to have more than a few cuts from glass shards. My mouth goes dry. I can see her back then. I go quiet and think about my own mortality and hers. I don't know what I'd do without Marie. I don't know why I picture her smashed up car when she's alright. I ask her why we put ourselves through imagining past events that make us feel uncomfortable. "Why do motorists crane their necks to look at accidents?"

"People want to feel." We are so unfeeling in our everyday lives as we rush about. We are taught to use our heads more than our hearts at work. I think people look at those less fortunate because it gives them reprieve from their own worries. We can feel better about our lives.

Marie makes me feel better as she says she takes less risks with driving now. "I'm more experienced and more responsible now I'm a parent," she comforts. I smile. Being a parent does make a lot of people think of others outside of their own difficulties. It's nice to care about others. The smashed avocado is a winner!

Pre-packed Salmon Sandwiches

I hate travelling backwards. I tell Marie that the little boy I look after has never been on a train. "Well, he loves buses. Maybe you could take him. A train should be smooth on your neck." This sounds like a good idea. I'm stuck in a chair every day on tablets. I could pace myself. "As long as there aren't salmon sandwiches," I say. She looks puzzled.

We talk about 'best before' and 'use by' dates. I always get them mixed up, I say. I don't really. I just like listening to Marie being the confident expert as I pretend to be helpless. It's a great way to flirt.

I was on a train once, coming home on leave, and a woman stank the carriage out with some supermarket sandwiches that were out of date. She was trying to describe the greyish salmon, over the phone, to customer services. Everyone was changing their seats as they held their noses. She opened the window. It was freezing on the train.

Marie wrinkled her nose. "I like trains," she said. "I like the feeling of not being in control. You have to totally trust the driver. There's nothing you can do if it crashes." I think about rollercoasters and shudder. I think about staying sober on nights out. "I like to be in control," I surmise. "Maybe your world is safer than mine." We talk about ontological security. How safe are we in the world? "It depends on your safety net," she says. "Whether you have people around you that are dependable." I think. I say that past experiences definitely shape how you react to adversity in the present. She agrees. Then she asks me why I'm smiling.

"It just sounds like something a woman would say. Enjoying the feeling of not being in control, on a train, as the scenery hurtles past. Is it a sexual thing?" Marie smiles. "Most things usually are," she winks.

Shepherd's Pie

I remember the first time I saw Marie since leaving school. It was dark when she finally parked in the street. It seemed to take forever as she had a long drive. I could hardly eat my Shepherd's Pie because I was so excited. Marie even had the confidence to pick me up from my Ex-partner's. We had texted and talked for almost two months over the phone.

I should have asked her what car she was driving as she announced, by text, she was here. I grabbed my bag of medications and felt anxious. I didn't want to tap on the wrong car window in darkness. She saw me first. The distance between us seemed longer than it was. My chest was somersaulting. We hugged after thirty years. I wanted to remember every detail.

Marie drove smoothly. She eased her clutch instead of snapping at it. I didn't even need to remind her about my neck. I asked her to turn the radio off. "Why?" I said that I wanted to focus on her with the least distractions. "You are funny!"

She parked in what was to be christened 'her parking spot' outside my flat. We held hands. We always do. "You looked like a Rock Star as you walked up the street," she remarked. I laughed and offered her a green tea. We put some music on and she kneeled down at my feet. I leaned forward and rubbed her slight back. I couldn't help laughing. "What are you laughing at?" I said I was just pleased to see her and that my mind was in neutral. "I wasn't thinking of anything," I said. Then, I laugh again. "A Rock Star? Well, what do I normally look like?" We laughed.

Carrot Cake

The chiropractor asked if we are married. Marie said we weren't. I smiled as I was able to remind Marie about her past medical history. "I'm not interrupting, am I?" Marie laughed despite her back ache.

Afterwards, she said she felt bubbles in her veins and had to walk about for a bit. I was pleased to walk, however awkward my legs were, as I'd sat through her hour of treatment. Marie said she could feel the benefits after just one session. We ordered carrot cake and shared some Dandelion and Burdock at an Art Installation cafe.

Then we watched a video in darkness. The screen projected large fingers with cardboard hands on each. They clapped like finger puppets. I wondered why I was restless. It was like not being able to sleep when Marie stayed with me. I wanted to be awake every moment as our time together was limited.

Marie was used to sleeping alone. So, we didn't cuddle all night. We held feet instead of hands so she had space and didn't get too hot. She no longer had to put a pillow between us to support her back. The chiropractor had been a really good experience and we felt intimate.

It always amazes me how Marie remembers song

lyrics. Then, as I'm recalling her history to the chiropractor's questions, I realise that I do listen. I just respond to the song's melodies more than the words. I do attend. But it depends on the context and the purpose. I switch off when listening to music. That's why I ask Marie to turn the car stereo off. I attend to her instead.

Beef Stew

"It's not my cup of tea," she texts as she later says she had mushrooms and fried eggs for tea. I know that you wouldn't eat beef stew. You're a vegetarian, I text. Later, she asks me why I left my partner. It was the little things, I reply.

"I'd have pulled the gate off its hinges and burned it," she says. I feel sad because I know Marie would do no such thing. She is being incongruous. I wouldn't even need to ask her to close the gate a second time. Even with her hands full of shopping bags, Marie would go back and shut the gate. It is different with her.

She listens and remembers. I do tidy up after Marie. But it's no hardship. I just like to be organised. I think that's from being in The Army. Marie still insists she'd have burned the gate.

"No! You would not." Marie texts some laughter faces. She is teasing me. I can't believe how tetchy I've been. I just know I listen more to her. I am older than I was. But I just give back what I receive. Marie has shown me love. And I have fed those loving acts with thoughtfulness.

The Full English

"I am absolutely gagging for a fried breakfast. Sausages, fried bread..." Marie laughs. Nothing else enters my mind as I help her with her coat. We head over to a cafe that takes me back to my truck driving days. I locate a squeezy bottle of mayonnaise and Marie finds a table. "They do vegetarian sausages," she beams. "Don't you like ketchup?" She knows I think tomato sauce is for girls. I growl like a man and she laughs.

The breakfasts are brought over and I am consumed by the extra-large plate full with three slices of toast on the side. I go straight for the black pudding, mushrooms and beans. I chew as a tension is relieved. I can taste it. My eyes are closed as I slowly savour my mouthful.

"Why do you love me?" I look at her. I smile. "You should never ask a serious question when a man is eating." I put my fork down and multi-task. It's not a distraction because I do love Marie. "I love our patience," I say. "We both have that." She smiles and listens.

"When you're outside, your dark brown hair looks almost ginger or red. You look so girly on bright summer days. It reminds me that you take risks and let your hair down sometimes. I love how youthful you look." She smiles.

"Then, sometimes when you wear your glasses, you look like a schoolteacher. Do you remember looking like a surgeon, in scrubs, with that apron you wear at work?" Marie nods and laughs.

"Well, you remind me about how responsible you are as a mother and at work. I can't believe you spin so many plates. You say I'm more laid back. But I'd wobble if I had to live your average day. You're an enigma." I think. "You're my star!"

I tell her that she is preferred without make-up and that I will love her no matter how she looks. "It comes from within." I tell her that eye liner almost makes her look oriental – or at least, Spanish. I talk about her face shapes and how long or round her cheekbones look at different angles. "You could pass for three or four different women."

I love her because she listens and second guesses what I'm thinking. Marie seems to be one step ahead of my needs or wants. She always has time for other people too.

I take a few mouthfuls of my breakfast as she beams. Then I talk about the time she video called me on the train. There was a noisy crowd of football supporters who intimidated an older lady by shouting and climbing on the seats. Marie wasn't afraid to confront them in a non-threatening manner. They calmed down before the conductor came. Then she reassured the lady. "I do fear that you'll come unstuck," I say. "But you do right not to ignore it." Too many people turn a blind eye nowadays.

"I also really love the ways you spend time with your kids. You teach them traditional things. I mean, you can easily afford to 'fob them off' but you don't. You bake, make jigsaws and craft. Your girls care about other children and they apply themselves instead of fritting their times away."

"They do have fun," she answers. "Yes. But they take a real interest in the environment and other's difficulties. They're beyond their years, really." Marie smiles. She smiles a big smile.

"I think I love your deep, dark eyes best of all. Do you know where my favourite place in the world is?" She shrugs and scoops up some beans. "Your left shoulder," We both laugh.

There is a happy silence as we eat. I tell her how I drifted through painful days for months. I talk about seeing everything brand new again and I talk about my writing. I love to write about the human condition; about social commentary but I'm also attracted to the escapism of horror. I just don't quite know how to marry the two. I don't want to be pigeon-holed. I want to write about anything that feels real, alive or...dead. I laugh.

"Ah! The Horror – yes!" She loves to listen to me talk about books. Marie says I come alive with my passions. "I know you say it comes from within but it's nice to have a muse," I reply.

She smiles again. "Marie! You don't need to worry about me. I have this knack of overcoming adversity because I have a strong faith. I believe in you too. You give me hope. And I'll always look out for you. I always will. As much as I can promise..."

There is a silence as we comfortably eat together. She passes the mayonnaise before I even reach for it. She knows that I love her. It's just nice to hear it sometimes. She can see how much I care by my purposes in life. Marie says, "actions speak louder." And it's true. I was bowled over by the milk-tray pillows and the trips out with the video calls. She always seems to choose the right presents too.

I love to scrub her back and brush her hair. I like to moisturise her legs and make her green tea. These are all acts of love. Sometimes though, it's just nice to hear "I love you." It's nice to hear words because words make things happen. We finish our breakfasts. I am stuffed but managed to finish the extra-large plate. "I think we'll skip puddings," she laughs.

Spinach

Marie gives me strength and convinced me to try spinach. I wrote her a poem:

Girl, 46

"Was your day OK?" It's just you
look away and I don't bee
line to your honey smooth
forehead. I don't see your worries -
those collected in blemishes or bags or
even uneven sags that I don't see.
You are not Exhibit A or B
or even C to be looked at like
a commodity. You are more,
my eternal amour. You
are my best sounding-board friend
and the perfect true love; my lover in dreams
and in each creamy rich chocolate
waking hour and day. The only
one with that timeless girl's heart – like
the laughter of bicycle rides -
and that sunrise smile as you nurture
other smiles around you.
You wear it loosely, care-free
as you 'pay it forward' or tightly tied
back on those few fraught long days.

Your happiest actions
outshine all that is outward
as they come from somewhere
softly ageless and inside. So,
let me now ask you, please.
You are important to me,
"Are you alright?"
"Was your day OK?"

Haddock and Chips

It's a lovely Summer evening so we head to the park with wrapped fish and chips. There are lots of dogs running free. I think people are more tolerant here. People in London would probably have their dogs on a tight leash. We get lots of "Hello's" and eye contact. Marie and I find a park bench overlooking a quiet football pitch.

"Did you order extra chips?" There is a mountain of them. The server didn't skimp on salt and vinegar either. I start laughing. "Bloody hell! That's a heart attack waiting to happen." Marie's eyes widen. The haddock is absolutely swimming in fat. It wasn't even drained from the deep fat fryer. She chuckles and says, "I think you're supposed to catch it first." We eat off the same white paper which is threatening to tear beneath the sodden fish.

Mitzi ambles over. She looks like a white Yorkshire Terrier. The owners vaguely called her but leave the dog to sniff at our tea. I'm not sure if to throw some chips on the grass. I ask Marie if I'm quite reserved. She smiles and strokes Mitzi. My fingers are really greasy. "I think you think about your actions on others," she replies.

At last, the owners call their dog. We look over the field onto the horizon. Marie nuzzles into my shoulder. "We can't just ride off into the sunset," she says. "We both have responsibilities." I feel sad. I'm going home early in the morning. I agree – although I'm trying to find a workable solution. There is silence. Then we find a bin for the daft amount of left-over chips and hold hands back to the car.

Macaroons

"We really should have had some tea," Marie says. I fall back onto the pillows trying to catch my breath. "Yes. But the macaroons were tasty." We have just made love again like we invented it. I feel like a teenager despite the aches. Marie has thought about everything.

The hotel room has a large window which overlooks the bar and eatery with a glass roof. I talk about listening to the rain on windows. "It's like being in the womb. I love being snuggled up in bed whilst listening to the rain on the window." Marie agrees. We make love again. Then cries as I moisturise her legs. "No-one has ever done that for me before," she says. "Well, you ordered the array of 'milk tray pillows' for my neck," I reply. I like to scrub her back in the bath too. I like to show her a maternal love as well as the more manly kind.

I cuddle Marie and she drifts off. I am too busy with my thoughts. The hotel room has oriental-like sliding doors to the bathroom and a writing table. I think about making a quick coffee. Marie awakes as the kettle boils. I make a coffee. She is grumpy as she stomps to the bathroom. "I'm not Jesus, you know," she barks, half asleep. Marie has to be up early for work.

I later ask her if she remembers that night. "Of

course! But I don't remember mentioning Jesus." I smile. "That hotel room had the world's loudest kettle."

Cheese and Ham Baguette

The first time it happened was on my very few trips into town. The short bus ride really makes my neck and arms sore. There's too much braking, swerving and accelerating and too many potholes. I don't enjoy going out. It's purely functional and I've had enough after two shops. I really can't browse CDs – the pains distract as it feels like I'm standing on Children's building bricks.

I am sat eating a ham and cheese baguette with a latte. I bite into the hard crust and then there's a shock. I wipe the sweat from my brow. I spit the tooth into the palm of my hand. My tongue searches for the new gap and I think about getting older. I finish my sandwich as I text Marie. "When did you last go to the dentist?" I frown. I am sweating more.

The second tooth presented itself on my tongue as I woke up at my children's house. It really freaks me out. Marie talks about flossing and black plaque. I buy some flossing tape but it doesn't become a habit because my arms hurt and the novelty soon wears off. "You should really go to the dentist," she says. I hadn't been for four years. I tell Marie that I'd rather saw my leg off.

I finally get to the dentist after a six weeks wait. Even for me, that is a long time not to see a specialist because I'm anxious about my tooth loss. I joke in the waiting room about the drill being a lawn mower outside. Something else in the clinic room sounds like a hedge strimmer. I wipe my brow. Marie is there, on the phone, to compliment me for being responsible.

A few days later, I am eating a chocolate bar that is cold and hard from being in the fridge. I feel my top left incisor free and covered in the chocolate I'm eating. I feel faint. It's the third tooth in as many months. Marie is incredulous. "At least you've still got a nice smile," she says. I brush my teeth more than once a day now.

Spiced Lentil Soup

I am in awe when Marie video calls me. She lives about four hours away in the car. Yesterday, she showed me the old trees in the deer park. The gnarly Oaks have been there far longer than we have. The phone reception isn't very good where she lives. I blame it on the space conkers.

I looked for other places of interest in her locality on the internet. There are some hills where a music festival takes a place and a village green where a film was shot. There are towns with cobbled streets and buildings with their own historical characters. Some of them are magpie houses.

She phones me today from the quarry I mentioned. She had forgotten about this beauty spot. Marie is glowing after the bike ride. The slight breeze is fanning her hair as the sun bounces off the brilliant white chalk. I am flabbergasted. "That is so thoughtful and romantic," I say.

Marie takes me everywhere with her video phone as I sit in my high-backed orthopaedic chair at home. "I must get back now," she smiles. "There's not many people about." It is quiet. I sit feeling warm and in love. What a romantic gesture!

She texts me after an age. I have been worrying because the country roads are perilous for cyclists.

She had popped to the Post Office on the way home and is now sat at her table with a bowl of spiced lentil soup. That memory has really stuck as it is steeped, as the hills, in a strong emotion.

Coleslaw Wrap

"You normally have to turn the oven on to cook," I laugh. Marie is so appreciative that someone has made her tea after work. "No-one has done that for ages," she says. We eat our wraps filled with coleslaw, cucumber and slices of cheese. Marie has her obligatory sweet chilli sauce. "Tell me what happened again," she continues.

"I've got Cervical Myelopathy but I didn't know. I went all through The Army without a glitch and worked in care for over twelve years. That's including working with people in Mental Health with The National Health Service. I was alright until I started running three years ago. Then I started getting pins and needles. I went to the doctor's. I went to the doctor's again. I thought it was residual stress or something psychosomatic. At last, the doctor sent me for an MRI. Then I got a phone call on a Friday afternoon. I couldn't take it in because of my pains and the shock."

"The doctor told me I had Cervical Myelopathy. I was born with it. It's congenital which means it happened at birth. My neck is too narrow in the middle and all the nerves seem to get sore. The pains affect my peripheral nervous system because the nerves run from the brain to my arms and legs through the narrow part in my neck."

I told her about the operation. I was so scared that I had arranged my will and a funeral plan. But on the day, I was trying not to watch morning television in the waiting room as I lay on the bed. They gave me oxygen. Then, five hours later, I woke up from swimming with dolphins, elsewhere, back on the ward. I was gagging for a brew. I tried to lift my head off the pillow but my neck felt really weak. I was wired and bandaged with a tube protruding from the front of where they'd removed two discs. There are two discs outstanding. One of the 'actioned' discs decompressed but the second one didn't. I just take it day-to-day. It's degenerative but I try to be positive." Marie tells me how strong I am. She says that she feels safe when I'm with her. That makes me feel stronger.

Vegetable Samosas

We have pet names but Marie knows I'm a private man. After she finishes work, I meet her outside with salad, vegetable samosas and her birthday Prosecco. I remember cutlery and two tumblers from my kitchen. She is pleased to see me.

We head to 'the Squirrel park' through narrow roads and heavy traffic. I turn her radio off. She's used to that by now. "Oh my goodness! I could have been raped today," I said. "It's a good job I didn't answer the door in the buff. I didn't think it was you." It was a diminutive old lady with glasses. She said, "I'm Linda" and burst in looking for a leak in the bathroom. She totally caught me by surprise.

Marie laughed as I continued to call her "Londa." It was a standing joke since Marie had texted 'Hoya' for 'Hi-ya' once. We managed to park eventually but the ticket machine required a PhD to enter the registration number and other details.

We laughed at the squirrel antics and tried to coax one with our cucumber. "I should have brought some nuts," I laughed. Apparently, if you drop nuts on hard standing, the squirrels come and get them. The park was sunny and busy. We ate our food then walked to the old remains. I felt really stiff as Marie pointed from the diagram on the board to where the pantry used to be. There wasn't much left of the castle now.

One of our favourite pictures was taken in 'the squirrel park.' Marie says she looks like an Elf and I look like a Giant at a festival. She takes really interesting photos.

A Chocolate Rabbit

It is round about Easter when Marie brings her daughters to visit at my flat. I struggle to open the carton of cranberry juice. "Are you struggling?" I tell Marie that I have become more clumsy as I drop things, stumble and feel stiff when it's cold. My pains are unbearable, at times too, and I sleep more because of the increased medications. "I'm alright," I say, "I'm a strong chap."

I pour the juice into tumblers for Katie and Joanne. They are always smiling and polite, I notice, from having said "Hello" a few times on video calls. Joanne hides behind her mam on the sofa whilst Katie talks about school and the Youth Club she attends. Marie's eldest is throwing and catching a bouncy ball as she talks. Joanne peeks out and takes some interest.

The ball has an iris printed on it. Katie catches the blood-shot eye. I joke about bouncing it off the ceiling. Marie mentions about how much of a person's eyeball must be hidden. I say it's like Isostasy in mountains. We only see the tip above ground. "There's a lot we don't see."

People don't see my pains. Sometimes, I wince or cry out but people either don't see it or choose not to. We can never really know what is going on in a person's life, below the surface, unless they choose to tell us. Marie can see that I'm deteriorating. I mask a lot but I'm a positive chap. The girls are full of life and make me laugh.

I find some Easter eggs I chose the day before and the girls are really appreciative. Marie gives me a chocolate rabbit. "Do you know what they do with the rabbits that don't get sold? They snap an ear off and cover them in Santa Claus foil." It was nice to see the kids at last.

Baklava

The last time I had a date with Marie was just before she visited with her children visited. Being a man, I didn't have enough toilet roll in so we passed through all the Saturday night revellers for our necessities. We were hungry too. I hadn't been to the Turkish restaurant since I took my kids on my birthday.

I was in pains but I felt like a Rock Star. I was also more than aware that Marie wasn't wearing any knickers. They were on my bedroom floor. It was freezing but she said, "I'm wearing stockings." We joked about one of the Mr. Men with long arms as we were seated near the window. Marie and I, tore through the vegetarian kebabs with rice and a side portion of chips.

Looking back, our selfie looks like we were on holiday. Marie is looking over her shoulder with a huge cocktail in view. The glass has brightly coloured straws and parasols which were in keeping with the Mediterranean decor of the restaurant. I had had my usual latte in a glass mug with a tiny handle. We had the sweetest Baklava afterwards. I can still taste the almonds and honey. What did we talk about? We mentioned horse racing and fox hunting. Some of the horses had been injured on television during The Steeplechase. I think the vegetarian option had prompted animal welfare chat again. Our last date was so varied and colourful with great food.

Nil by Mouth

I am on peg-feed now. I don't really have any concept of night or day. It's more a fleeting timelessness. Sometimes, I feel like I am floating but beyond that, I can't feel any sensations, even when I'm being bathed or hoisted. I am only anchored to this life by the weight of my memories now.

I think I can smell Marie's favourite scent. But is her perfume a memory as she brushes her fingers through my hair? I only know she's trying to comfort me because she is giving one of her commentaries. "I am stroking your hair and thinking about our lives." I listen to her. Listening is all I can do. It hurts that I can't communicate or tell her "I love you." I'm just lucky that she spends time with me in my bedroom that I can't see.

She tells me that she remembers that I went to Canada, with The Army, and fed gophers some biscuits on the sub-zero prairie. She says how brave I am to have driven a wagon through cross-country snow. I feel happy but I can't raise a smile.

She talks about how we each juggled separate University studies whilst raising young children. "That's temerity," she says. Then she is laughing about the time we had to nip out, late at night, for a plaster. "The garage forecourt assistant must have thought we wanted contraceptives at that hour." I feel happy but I can't convey that.

Marie sings our favourite songs and reads from children's books. Then after I try to follow the competitive Squirrels, that finally learn to share, she might read an excerpt from a novel I like. She has all the time in her world.

She knows me well enough to know that I'd still want to share my experiences. It hurts me that I can't communicate that. But I'm happy that she persists and keeps me updated. Marie knows me well.

Marie talks about what she has eaten and what the girls are doing. Joanne volunteers with Rescue Animals and is studying a Veterinary Degree. Her eldest, Katie, is still happily finding her feet. "Have you 'seen' your Girls?" I can't answer her. But my eldest talks to Marie and keeps her up to date on their visits and my health. My children keep me safe in this disappearing life.

Marie sings. She sings until it's time to go. She kisses me, pulls her coat on, and I drift until her next visit.

Angel Delight

I feel weightless as I head towards the pinprick of light that grows brighter and wider until it engulfs me. My smile gets bigger as the last of the pain melts and I am weightless. It is all bright. The brightest.

I look for the narrow gate. But he asks me softly, "What difference did you make?" I felt confident. "I loved and acknowledged others." He smiled. He saw what is in my heart and told me to return another day. I visit my girls. I go to Marie.

She is sobbing at her kitchen table. She looks so small because I am not governed by material laws. It would have broken my heart before. But now I am no longer following the same rules. She blows her nose. Marie dries her reddened eyes. She looks confused. I whisper. I whisper but she cannot hear me on an auditory level.

Marie senses something and smiles. She laughs. Then she gets up from her chair and goes straight to her car keys. "I knew they were there all along," she tells Katie. Then I wait for her. But it doesn't feel like waiting.

Also from Red Cape Publishing

Anthologies:

Elements of Horror Book One: Earth
Elements of Horror Book Two: Air
Elements of Horror Book Three: Fire
Elements of Horror Book Four: Water
A is for Aliens: A to Z of Horror Book One
B is for Beasts: A to Z of Horror Book Two
C is for Cannibals: A to Z of Horror Book Three
D is for Demons: A to Z of Horror Book Four
E is for Exorcism: A to Z of Horror Book Five
F is for Fear: A to Z of Horror Book Six
G is for Genies: A to Z of Horror Book Seven
H is for Hell: A to Z of Horror Book Eight
It Came From The Darkness: A Charity Anthology

Short Story Collections:

Embrace the Darkness by P.J. Blakey-Novis
Tunnels by P.J. Blakey-Novis
The Artist by P.J. Blakey-Novis
Karma by P.J. Blakey-Novis
The Place Between Worlds by P.J. Blakey-Novis
Home by P.J. Blakey-Novis
Short Horror Stories by P.J. Blakey-Novis
Short Horror Stories Volume 2 by P.J. Blakey-Novis
Keep It Inside by Mark Anthony Smith
Everything's Annoying by J.C. Michael

Novelettes:

The Ivory Tower by Antoinette Corvo

Novellas:

Four by P.J. Blakey-Novis
Dirges in the Dark by Antoinette Corvo
*The Cat That Caught The Canary by Antoinette
Corvo*
*Bow-Legged Buccaneers from Outer Space by
David Owain Hughes*

Novels:

Madman Across the Water by Caroline Angel
The Curse Awakens by Caroline Angel
Less by Caroline Angel
Where Shadows Move by Caroline Angel
The Broken Doll by P.J. Blakey-Novis
*The Broken Doll: Shattered Pieces by P.J.
Blakey-Novis*
The Vegas Rift by David F. Gray

Children's Books:

*Grace & Bobo: The Trip to the Future by Peter
Blakey-Novis*
The Little Bat That Could by Gemma Paul
The Mummy Walks at Midnight by Gemma Paul
A Very Zombie Christmas by Gemma Paul

Follow Red Cape Publishing

www.redcapepublishing.com
www.facebook.com/redcapepublishing
www.twitter.com/redcapepublish
www.instagram.com/redcapepublishing
www.pinterest.co.uk/redcapepublishing
www.patreon.com/redcapepublishing

Printed in Great Britain
by Amazon

62993129R00059